F
HIS   Hiser, Constance

           The missing doll

THE
MISSING DOLL

Other Books by Constance Hiser

CRITTER SITTERS
DOG ON THIRD BASE
GHOSTS IN FOURTH GRADE
NO BEAN SPROUTS, PLEASE!
SCOOP SNOOPS
SIXTH-GRADE STAR

THE MISSING DOLL

Constance Hiser

drawings by Marcy Ramsey

HOLIDAY HOUSE / NEW YORK

Library of Congress Cataloging-in-Publication Data

Hiser, Constance.
The missing doll / by Constance Hiser : drawings by Marcy Ramsey.
—1st ed.
p.   cm.
Summary: Abby buys a one-of-a-kind doll that not only tells her
answers to her homework and what is for dinner, but also helps her
find a fourth-grade classmate who is in trouble.
ISBN 0-8234-1046-3
[1. Dolls—Fiction. 2. Magic—Fiction. 3. Friendship—Fiction.]
I. Ramsey, Marcy Dunn, ill. II. Title.
PZ7.H618Mi   1993   93-807   CIP
[Fic]—dc20   AC

Contents

THE
MISSING DOLL

Chapter One

The Talking Doll

"Imagine, a toy shop opening in Cedar Grove, just in time for your birthday!" Heather said, as the three girls rode their bikes beneath the tall elm trees on Robin Lane. "This is such a little town, I wonder who would want to open a store here?"

"It surprised me, too, when I saw the sign yesterday," Abby admitted. "But I

3

think it's terrific. It might be weeks before Mom and Dad go to the city, and I want to spend my birthday money *right now*. I hope the new shop has those whistling hula hoops they show on TV. I think that's what I want."

"How much money do you have to spend, Abby?" asked her younger sister Sandy, shouting because she was lagging behind the others. She was too little to pedal as fast as they did.

"Eighteen dollars and fifty-six cents," Abby shouted back proudly. "Mom and Dad gave me fifteen dollars, and I also have three dollars and fifty-six cents left over from last month's allowance."

"Wow!" Sandy exclaimed. "I bet you can buy something neat with that. I wish *I* had some money."

"You will," said Heather. "Your birthday comes in July, doesn't it? That's only three months away. You'll have your turn then."

"That seems like a long time from now,"

Sandy pouted. "I wanted to go shopping today."

"There it is!" Abby broke in. "See, it's that little house where old Mrs. Hartnell used to live. Isn't that a cute sign out front?"

Heather and Sandy stared at the heart-shaped wooden sign, decorated with flowers and ribbons.

"Heart's Desire," Heather read. "That's a funny name for a toy store."

Abby shrugged. "I guess so," she said. "But that's what it is, all right. I looked in the front window yesterday, and there were shelves of dolls and teddy bears and games. What else could it be but a toy store? What are we waiting for? Let's go in!"

The girls scrambled off their bikes and dropped them on the soft new grass in the front lawn of the little brown house. Then they raced each other down the short brick walk and up the steps to the narrow porch.

"Ring the bell," said Heather.

"We don't have to," Abby answered, pointing to a sign on the front door. "See? It says, 'Open—Come In.'"

The three girls pushed against the door and stepped into a small, square room. Three sides of the room were lined with long shelves, filled with stacks of games, stuffed animals, and dolls of all kinds. There were ballerina dolls in fluffy pink tutus, Japanese dolls in long, embroidered kimonos, clown dolls with red noses and orange wigs, and bride dolls with white satin dresses, flowing lace veils, and tiny flower bouquets.

"I've never seen so many dolls in my life," Heather whispered. "I don't see any hula hoops, though."

"Maybe they're in one of the other rooms," Abby answered. She whispered, too, even though she didn't really know why. "I wonder if anyone's here. They wouldn't just go off and leave the shop unlocked, would they?"

6

"Shh," Sandy said, "I think I hear someone coming."

Sure enough, a moment later all three
girls heard the busy *tap-tap-tap* of shoes
coming down the hallway toward them.
There was another sound, too. It sounded
like the soft ringing of dozens of tiny silver
bells. The red curtain in the hall doorway
parted, and the strangest figure they had
ever seen stepped into the room.

"It's a princess!" Sandy whispered. "Just
like in my book of fairy tales!"

Abby wasn't sure about that, but the
woman who stood there smiling at them
did look exactly like one of the princesses
in Sandy's book. She was tall and slender,
and her golden hair was as bright as sunshine. Her dress floated below her knees
in folds of wispy white and pink and blue.
Pink and blue ribbons laced the front of
the bodice, dancing every time she moved.
And yes, there were dozens and dozens of
tiny silver bells sewn all over the woman's
skirts, jingling softly as she walked. Her

eyes were as blue as a morning sky, and she was staring at Abby's head, as if she could read the thoughts inside.

"Welcome," she said in a soft, sweet voice. "Welcome to Heart's Desire. May you find exactly what you want most here."

"H-heart's Desire?" Abby repeated, her voice quavering just a little. "Why do you call your shop Heart's Desire?"

Once again the woman smiled. "Every toy here is waiting to be someone's best friend," she explained. "And when you have found a friend, what is there left for your heart to desire? With a true friend, you have everything."

The girls glanced quickly at each other. This woman seemed stranger by the minute.

"I see," Abby said. "That's very interesting. Do you have any hula hoops? My birthday was yesterday, and—"

"And you came to buy one of my beautiful dolls." The woman's smile got even bigger. "I know there's one here that will be just right for you. Let's see, which one shall it be?" She turned toward the shelves of dolls.

"I don't want a doll," Abby answered. "What I really came in for—"

The woman waved one hand, as if she were shooing away a fly. "I think I have the very one for you," she said. "Yes, here she is, right here."

Taking a large doll from the top shelf, she fluffed out its full white, pink, and blue skirts and smoothed its long golden hair. "Here," she said, holding the doll out toward the girls, "this is the doll for you."

The girls stared. "But—" Heather exclaimed. "But it's *you!*"

Sure enough, the doll looked almost exactly like the shopkeeper, right down to the silver bells on her skirts.

"But of course," the woman said. "Desiree is my very own creation. And she

9

knows you already, or my name isn't Emily Moonbow. See the way she's smiling at you?"

"Desiree?" Sandy wrinkled up her nose. "What kind of name is that?"

Emily Moonbow laughed. "It means someone who is wanted very much," she explained. "The way the young lady wants her now, yes?"

"But I *don't* want her," Abby said. "I mean—well, she's a beautiful doll, maybe the most beautiful doll I've ever seen. But what I really want is a hula hoop. After all, I'm in fourth grade, and I'm a little old for dolls."

Emily Moonbow clucked her tongue. "Who could ever be too old for a new friend?" she asked. "Besides, this doll is special. This doll talks. She says some amazing things."

"Really?" Abby looked more closely at the doll. "Oh, yeah, I see the string you pull. What kind of things does she say?"

The woman shrugged. "That will be for

you to discover," she answered. "Once the two of you are friends, who knows what she'll have to tell you?"

"Oh, come on," Heather protested, "they make thousands of those dolls in some factory, all just alike. They probably all say the same things."

But the shopkeeper shook her head. "Not Desiree," she answered. "Remember, I told you that she is my own creation. This doll is a genuine, one-of-a-kind Friendship Doll. There's not another like her anywhere in the whole world."

A Friendship Doll! Abby reached out one finger to stroke the doll's filmy skirts. In spite of herself, she was almost beginning to want the doll. "That settles it, anyway," she said with a sigh. "A doll like that must cost a lot of money. I don't have that much to spend."

"Oh?" Emily Moonbow tilted her head to one side, like a curious bird. "How much do you have?"

"Exactly eighteen dollars and fifty-six

cents," Abby told her. "Not nearly enough for—"

"What a coincidence!" the woman cried. "That happens to be exactly the price of this doll!"

The girls stared at her. "Are you sure?" Abby asked. "That doesn't seem like much for a one-of-a-kind doll."

"I know the price of everything in my shop," the woman said firmly. "And the price of that doll is eighteen dollars and fifty-six cents. Exactly."

Abby's mouth stretched into a delighted grin. "That's terrific!" she said. "I'll take her!"

Heather poked her friend. "Hey, what about your hula hoop?" she reminded her.

"Yeah," Sandy agreed. "And just last month you gave me all your dolls. You said you were too old for them."

"That was last month," Abby said. "Besides, who wants a boring old hula hoop, when they can have a one-of-a-kind talking Friendship Doll?"

"Well, at least listen to her *say* something before you make up your mind," Heather insisted. "You ought to make sure she works."

"I'll demonstrate," Emily Moonbow said, pulling the ring at the back of the doll's neck. "Although she probably won't have anything important to say until she gets to know you better."

There was a tiny humming sound, and then a voice that came from the doll's mouth: "I'm Desiree, I'm a real Friendship Doll—and I've chosen *you* for my best friend of all!"

Abby's mouth dropped open. "She talks in rhyme!" she said.

"All the best dolls do." Emily Moonbow smiled. "That will be eighteen dollars and fifty-six cents, please. Enjoy your new friend—and listen closely. She might say something you need to hear."

"What was all that about?" Heather wondered, as the girls pedaled back along Robin Lane, with Abby's new doll cradled carefully in her bicycle basket. "What could a doll say that you need to hear? Everyone knows those dolls say the same five or six things, over and over and over. If you ask me, that woman is *weird*."

"Yeah," Sandy agreed, "she's *spooky*."

"But you have to admit, this really is a beautiful doll," Abby insisted, admiring the doll's tiny pearl earrings. "And she's a lot more interesting than a hula hoop."

"If you say so," Heather grumbled. "All I know is, that Emily Moonbow is some saleswoman. You didn't even want to buy a doll when you went in there. Now, all of a sudden, you're nuts over it. I still think there's something strange about the whole thing."

Abby just laughed as they turned their bikes toward Willow Street. No matter what Heather thought, Desiree was the most beautiful doll Abby had ever seen.

And there wasn't another doll like her in the whole wide world.

Chapter Two

The Birthstone Ring

Abby was playing with Desiree—Desi, for short—on Saturday afternoon when she noticed that her birthstone ring was missing.

It wasn't just any birthstone ring. It was the ring her grandmother had given her for Christmas just a few months ago. Abby hardly ever took it off, except when she

was taking a bath or helping with the supper dishes.

"No!" she gasped, looking down at her bare finger. "Not my ring! Where in the world could I have put it?"

"What's the matter?" asked Sandy, looking up from her spelling workbook. "Don't tell me you already broke your new doll."

"It's my ring!" Abby answered, feeling tears prickle at the backs of her eyes. "My beautiful birthstone ring! Oh, Sandy, what will I do if I can't find it? What will I tell Grandma?"

"It's okay." Her little sister laid down her pencil and stood up, brushing off the seat of her jeans. "I'll help you look for it. Where were you today? Weren't you outside helping Mom in the garden this morning?"

Abby's hand flew to her mouth. "That's it! I bet I lost it when I was weeding in the tulip bed. Oh, Sandy, if it fell in all that mud, we may never find it!"

The two girls rushed outside, leaving Abby's doll propped up in one corner of the couch. The screen door slammed behind them as they flew down the porch steps and across the lawn toward Mom's flower bed. Her prize pink and yellow tulips swayed in a cool April breeze.

"Be careful," Abby warned her little sister as they bent over the flowers. "If we squash Mom's flowers, she'll squash *us*. Oh, Sandy, I don't see it anywhere, do you?"

"Not yet," her sister answered, getting down on her hands and knees to peer through the thick green leaves. "But we just got here. Don't worry, Abby, we'll find your ring."

But fifteen minutes later, even Sandy had to admit that the birthstone ring was nowhere in the flower bed.

"Okay, so where else were you today?" she asked as she brushed one hand across her forehead, leaving a streak of mud behind. "When's the last time you saw your ring?"

Abby thought hard. "Let's see, I know I

had it on at breakfast. I got maple syrup on it and had to wipe it off. Then I helped Mom with the dishes—wait! I'll bet that's it. I bet I left it on the counter beside the kitchen sink. I always take it off when I wash dishes."

But the ring wasn't on the kitchen counter. It wasn't in Abby's closet, or tangled in the blankets on her bed, or under the cushions of the living room couch. An hour later, Abby and her sister had searched everywhere they could think of, but there was no sign of Abby's ring.

"Maybe Mom found it and put it away," Sandy suggested. "We can ask her when she and Dad get back from the store."

"But that won't be for hours yet." Abby sighed. "They were going to Aunt Wilda's house, too, remember? If I have to worry about my ring that long, I'll go crazy. Besides, I was hoping I could find it before Mom got back, so she wouldn't have to know I lost it. She's always telling me not to be so careless with my things."

19

"Well, *I* don't know where else to look," Sandy said. "And it's not like I don't have anything else to do today. Give it up for now, Abby. Your ring will turn up sooner or later."

"Maybe not," Abby said, beginning to cry, "maybe it's lost forever!"

She didn't even try to blink back the tears as she plopped down on the couch and picked up her new doll, hugging it tightly to her chest.

"I wish you really *did* know how to talk," she said. "Maybe you could tell me where my ring is."

Sandy snorted. "Come on," she said, "you've had that doll for three whole days, and she's never said anything interesting. It's like Heather said—she just says the same stuff over and over. Hey, I think I'll go to the kitchen for a snack. You want to come?"

Abby shook her head. "My stomach hurts too much to eat anything."

Sandy shrugged. "Suit yourself. But I

happen to know Mom baked a whole batch of peanut butter cookies last night."

She disappeared into the kitchen, leaving Abby alone with her doll on the couch.

"I bet you *could* help me find my ring, Desi," Abby whispered, hugging her doll. "If you could really talk, that is."

She wiped her tears from her cheeks with the back of one hand and tugged at the string on Desi's neck. There was a soft humming noise, and then the doll's mechanical voice.

"Out where the flowers grow, deep in the shade—look in the place where your wishes are made."

Abby stared at her doll. "That's a new one," she said. "And it doesn't make a lot of sense to me. What a weird thing for a doll to say."

She gasped and jumped to her feet, still clutching the doll.

"Sandy!" she yelled. "Sandy, come quick! I know where my ring is!"

Sandy rushed into the living room, her

cheeks bulging with cookies. "Where?" she asked, spraying peanut butter crumbs.

"Just follow me!" Abby cried, hurrying through the front door and down the porch steps.

Her heart beat hard as she led her sister across the lawn toward the tulip patch.

"But we've already looked there!" Sandy protested.

"We looked in the flower bed," Abby agreed. "But we didn't think about Mom's little pretend wishing well."

Sure enough, the afternoon sunshine sparkled on something on the edge of the small stone-and-concrete wishing well that stood behind the tulips near the tall maple tree. It wasn't a real well—there wasn't even any water in it—but the girls liked to pretend that it was a wishing well, and that it could make their favorite wishes come true.

"It's my ring!" Abby said, laughing triumphantly as she scooped it up from the rim of the well. "I remember now—I was

afraid I'd get it all muddy, working in the flower bed, so I put it up here. I forgot all about it, until—"

"Until what?" Sandy asked, staring at her curiously.

Abby stared back at her little sister. If she told her about what Desi had said, Sandy would probably laugh. Anyone would. After all, it wasn't as if a doll could really find a lost ring. The whole thing was probably just a coincidence. "Look in the place where your wishes are made. . . ."

"Until I just remembered, that's all," she finished lamely. "Uh, let's go back in, Sandy. I think I feel like a snack after all."

Just coincidence, she told herself again. That's all it could be.

Chapter Three

Really Weird

In the next few days it grew harder and harder for Abby to ignore the weird things Desi said. How do you ignore a doll that helps you with your homework? "Seven times seven will turn out just fine, if you first write a four, and then write a nine," Desi said, when Abby was having trouble learning the sevens multiplication table.

And how about a doll that gives you the supper menu? "Meat loaf and potatoes, string beans and pie, plus a choice of hot dinner rolls, whole wheat or rye," Desi said on Monday evening, just as Abby was about to wander into the kitchen to ask Mom what was for supper. Abby hadn't even realized she had pulled the doll's string until that scratchy voice came out. And sure enough, supper was meat loaf, mashed potatoes, string beans, chocolate cream pie, and hot rolls.

It was weird, all right, so weird that Abby didn't tell anyone about it, not even Sandy or Heather. They'd probably think she was loony. Sometimes Abby even wondered about it herself.

She decided to go back to Heart's Desire and ask Emily Moonbow about the strange things Desi was saying. But the afternoon she went there, the toy store was closed. At least, the front door wouldn't open, no matter how hard she tugged, and no one came when she rang the doorbell. Maybe

Really Weird

Emily Moonbow was out buying groceries, Abby thought. She'd have to come back some other day.

In the meantime, strange things kept happening. It seemed that every time she lost something, or had a problem with her homework, or forgot one of her friends' telephone numbers, the Friendship Doll had the answer, just as soon as Abby remembered to pull her string. Sometimes the things the doll said took a little figuring out, like her rhyme about the wishing well, but as soon as Abby thought about them a little, everything Desi said made sense.

In the next three or four days, Desi told her to be sure to use cold water when she washed her new pink sweater, to take the cookies out of the oven because they were about to burn, and to remember to buy a birthday card for her dad. "I'll never forget anything," Abby said to her doll one day. "You're better than tying a string around my finger."

But the weirdest thing happened on Friday morning, when Abby caught Julie Wise copying her homework. Abby had suspected for days that someone was going through her desk before school every day and copying her homework. It wasn't hard to figure out. In the morning, as soon as Abby got to school, she put her homework neatly in her desk, then hurried outside to play on the jungle gym with Heather until the first bell rang. And every morning, when she went back inside and took her homework out of her desk, the papers were just a little crumpled, the pencil lines just a little smudged. Someone must be copying her homework—but who?

On Thursday evening, while Abby sat at the desk in her bedroom doing her math, she was thinking about the homework thief. Her doll sat on the back of the desk, smiling her dimpled smile and looking mysterious. "Too bad you don't go to school, Desi," Abby said, straightening the doll's skirts. "This wouldn't be much of a puzzle for you."

She pulled the doll's string and heard the usual soft humming, and then Desi spoke, loud and clear: "She copies your homework, as quick as a wink, look for the thief who is dressed all in pink."

Abby almost dropped the doll, she was so shocked. "Julie Wise!" she gasped. "Who else could it be?"

Julie Wise always wore *something* pink, even if it was just a hair ribbon. Pink was Julie's favorite color, as she reminded everyone in class about a million times a day. Julie wasn't exactly Abby's favorite person. She was too bossy on the playground, and she never took turns on the swings. But Abby never would have thought she was a thief.

Just to make sure, on Friday morning, Abby put her homework in her desk, then hid in the supply closet instead of going out to the playground. She kept the door open just a crack. Five minutes later, she saw

Julie tiptoeing into the classroom. Julie looked all around to make sure she was alone, then took the papers from Abby's desk, sat down, and began to copy them.

"You dirty sneak!" Abby yelled, bouncing out of the closet. "Why don't you do your own homework?"

Julie tried to be snippy about it, but she knew she had been caught red-handed.

"Well, that's one mystery solved," Abby reported to her doll that night. "I bet Julie Wise won't be stealing anyone's homework again for a while. Hey, Desi, you wouldn't happen to know a good recipe for cookies, would you? Heather's coming over to spend the night, and Mom said we could make some."

On Saturday evening, Abby's parents said the girls could stay up to watch the late, late show as a special treat. Sandy watched with them, but she kept nodding off, until she finally fell asleep just before midnight, right there in the middle of the living room floor.

"This is a boring movie anyway," Heather said with a yawn. "Do you think your mom would mind if we make those cookies now?"

"Not if we're careful," said Abby, switching off the TV. "Besides, we can always wake up my parents if there's a problem. You look through the cookbook and pick a recipe, and I'll see if we have all the ingredients."

Five minutes later, the girls had most of the ingredients for Double Chocolate Peanut Butter Cookies laid out on the kitchen counter.

"But we need more sugar," Abby said, checking the sugar canister. "Mom keeps an extra sack in the storeroom downstairs in the basement. I'll go down and get some."

"No, I will," Heather answered. "I know where your mom keeps stuff. Why don't you start measuring the cocoa?"

"Okay." Abby got Mom's big measuring cup. "Oh, Heather, wait—you'd better turn on the light before you start down the basement stairs. They're pretty steep."

"But the light switch is outside your back door, and I don't want to have to go out in the rain," Heather argued. "I don't know why anyone would put that switch in such an out-of-the-way place."

"Oh, you know how it is with old houses," said Abby as she poured cocoa into the measuring cup. "Dad says people keep building additions onto them, and sometimes the rooms turn out funny. Anyway, you ought to turn on the light."

"Don't worry," Heather said, opening the door that led to the basement steps. "There's plenty of light right here in the kitchen. I can see okay until I get to the bottom of the steps. Then I'll turn on the light in the storeroom."

"*You* tell her, okay, Desi?" Abby joked, picking up her doll from the kitchen table and pulling the string.

A chill seemed to chase itself down Abby's backbone as the doll chimed, "Be-

33

ware, beware, there is danger down there. Someone could get hurt if she doesn't take care!"

Heather's eyes bulged. "*What?*" she breathed. "What was all *that* about, Abby?"

Abby shook her head, still staring at the doll. "I don't know," she admitted, "but I think we'd better go outside and turn on that light."

A minute later, as they stood at the top of the basement stairs, the girls understood. One of Sandy's roller skates lurked on the stairs, about halfway down.

Abby swallowed hard. "Gosh, Heather," she gulped, "if you had stepped on that in the dark—"

"Don't say it," Heather interrupted. Her face had turned a funny green color, even her freckles. Suddenly she sat down hard on the top step. "What's going on here anyway, Abby? Something tells me you know a lot more than you've been letting on."

"I guess I'd better tell you everything,"

Abby agreed. "But stick with me, Heather. You're never going to believe this."

It took a long time for her to tell Heather all the weird things that had happened since she had bought the Friendship Doll. Heather didn't laugh, not even once. She just kept looking at Desi with eyes that got wider and wider, especially when Abby told her about Julie Wise and the stolen homework.

"This is the strangest thing that's ever happened in Cedar Grove," Heather said, when Abby was finally finished. "You do realize what this means, don't you? That weird woman at the toy store sold you some kind of magic doll."

"Magic?" Abby laughed a shaky laugh. "I don't know if there's such a thing as magic, Heather."

"Oh, yeah?" Heather sounded almost mad. "Well, what else would you call it? You ought to go back to the toy store and make that Emily Moonbow give you an explanation."

35

"I tried that," Abby admitted. "In fact, I've tried two or three times. But there's never anyone there, and the shop is always locked."

"Well, I think we should try again, just as soon as we get the chance," Heather insisted. "Because there's definitely something going on here, and we need to get to the bottom of it. I have to tell you, Abby, I have goose bumps clear to the soles of my feet!"

"Do you still want to make those cookies?" Abby asked after a long, silent minute.

"I guess so," Heather answered, getting to her feet. "I'll go downstairs for that sugar now. And I think I'll move Sandy's skate while I'm at it."

"Good idea," Abby agreed. "I'd hate for you to break your neck now."

A few minutes later, the girls were measuring and mixing at the kitchen table. But every few minutes, when they looked up and saw Desi's big blue eyes staring at them, they exchanged looks and got very quiet.

Heather was right. This was the weirdest thing that had ever happened in Cedar Grove.

Chapter Four

Missing!

Abby hummed a little song as she, Sandy, and Heather pedaled their bikes up the long country road, toward the crossroads where the school building loomed over the fields like a red, brick giant. Abby had told Miss Applegate about her new doll, and her teacher had suggested she bring it in and show it to the class. After all, how

38

many people had a real, genuine, one-of-a-kind Friendship Doll?

Desi rode in Abby's bike basket, and Abby glanced at the doll once in a while, admiring the way her long golden hair flowed in the breeze, and the way all of those tiny silver bells tinkled when the bike hit a bump in the road.

The second Abby got to school, she was surrounded by a group of *oohing, aahing* girls who all wanted to stroke Desi's filmy skirts and the bright pink and blue ribbons on her dress. All of them asked where they could get a doll like Desi, until Abby explained proudly that she was a one-of-a-kind. "There's not another one like her anywhere in the world!" she finished, and she and Heather exchanged mysterious glances. No one but the two of them knew how special Desi really was!

Abby's proud and happy mood lasted all through the spelling test (an A) and all through morning recess. She took Desi out to the playground with her, and once more

she was surrounded. Even the fifth and sixth graders wanted to see the wonderful doll. Abby had never felt so popular.

She didn't pull Desi's string, though. Who knew what the doll might say, or what might happen if she said something really weird?

After lunch, the class had to go downstairs to the cafeteria for music class. "You'd better leave your doll here," Miss Applegate told Abby. "She'll be just fine sitting on top of your desk."

Abby was still humming "America, the Beautiful" when she came back to the classroom thirty minutes later. But the hum stuck in her throat when she saw her empty desktop. Where was Desi?

Maybe she fell under the desk, Abby thought frantically, bending down to look. But the doll wasn't there, or on the bookshelf, or in the big wastebasket by Miss Applegate's desk.

"Don't worry," the teacher told her, "we'll all help you find your doll. She has to be here someplace. Maybe the custodian put her somewhere else for safekeeping."

But Mr. O'Connell hadn't seen Abby's doll. Neither had Mrs. Winters, the principal. And, although the whole fourth grade spent every minute until the last recess searching all through the classroom, there was no sign of Desi anywhere. She had vanished.

"But I have to find her," Abby said, sobbing. "I'll never get another doll like Desi— she's the only one anywhere."

"Try not to worry too much," Miss Applegate said, gently wiping a stray tear from Abby's cheek. "We know she didn't get up and walk away. And there aren't that many places in the school for a doll to hide. We'll find her, wait and see. If not today, then tomorrow for sure."

Abby cried all the way home, while Heather and Sandy rode long-faced and silent beside her.

"Don't cry, Abby," Sandy said at last,

"you can borrow my teddy bear. Or I'll let you have your old Suzi Sunshine doll back."

"It wouldn't be the same," Abby said. "Thanks, Sandy, but don't you understand? It just wouldn't be the same at all!"

The three girls were very quiet the rest of the way home.

Chapter Five

Nothing but a Thief

"I've got to find that doll!" Abby insisted. She and Heather were on the playground for afternoon recess on Tuesday, but this time they hadn't swung on the swings, or climbed on the monkey bars, or spun on the merry-go-round. They had spent this whole recess poking under every bush, and in back of every trash can, and inside

44

each hollow tree on the playground, looking for Abby's doll. "Desi's not an ordinary doll. She's a magic doll. And she's *my* doll. I want her back."

Heather sighed, leaning her chin wearily on her hands. "I know you do," she said, "but what else can we do? We've looked all over the school, and all over the playground, too. There's no place left to search. If Desi were still anywhere around, we would have found her by now."

"Not necessarily," Abby said stubbornly. "I've got an idea that someone took my doll, just to be nasty. What's more, I think I know exactly who it was, too."

"Who?" Heather demanded.

Abby crossed her arms over her chest and glared across the playground toward the swings, where a faded pink sweatshirt flashed up and down, up and down, as the swing rose and fell.

Heather looked in the direction of her glare. "You mean Julie Wise?" she gasped. "But why would—Oh, I get it. Because you

45

caught her copying your homework the other day, right?"

"Exactly," Abby nodded. "She knows how much I love that doll, and this is just her little way of getting even. But she's not going to get away with it. I'm going to get my doll back, no matter what I have to do."

"But how?" Heather asked. "You can't just ring Julie's doorbell and tell her to give your doll back. She'd say she didn't have it, and then what would you do, call the police to search her house?"

"Well, I'm not going to let her keep my doll," Abby snapped. "And I won't need the police to get her back, either. As a matter of fact, that's where you come in, Heather."

"Me?" Heather squeaked. "What do I have to do with it?"

Abby leaned toward her friend and spoke in a low voice. "I happen to know that there's a high school game tonight in Cherry Junction. And I also happen to know that one of Julie's big brothers is on the team. Don't ask me which brother—Julie has so many, I can never keep track of them."

"Yeah," Heather agreed. "I think there are ten kids in Julie's family, or maybe it's eleven, since her new sister was born. How do you suppose it would *feel* to have that many brothers and sisters?"

"Never mind that," Abby interrupted. "Who cares how Julie feels, anyway? She's nothing but a thief, and I want my doll back."

"So what's the big plan?" Heather asked. "And what's the baseball game got to do with anything?"

Abby grinned. "I bet Julie's whole family goes to that game tonight," she said. "Julie's always talking about her brother and his dumb old ball games, remember? That will give us a perfect chance to search for my doll."

"Whoa!" Heather was shaking her head very fast. "Count me out. I don't like the idea of sneaking around in someone else's house. We could get in trouble. We could even get arrested for breaking and entering."

"Who says we'll have to break in?" Abby argued. "Maybe they'll leave a window open or something. And it's not like we'd really be doing anything wrong. After all, Julie stole my doll. All I want to do is get her back."

"But you don't even know Julie is the thief!" Heather reminded her. "Not for sure."

Abby glared again at the pink sweatshirt on the other side of the playground. "Who else would it be?" she demanded. "Julie Wise is the only person I know who's rotten enough to steal my doll. Besides, she's been looking at me funny ever since the day I caught her copying my homework. It is Julie—I know it is. Come on, Heather, you have to help me look for Desi."

"Absolutely not," said Heather, sticking her lower lip out. "I refuse to let you talk me into such a dangerous stunt."

49

"I'll give you my jewelry box," Abby coaxed.

Heather looked up. "You mean the one with the ballerina on top? Wow, Abby, that's—No! I know what you're trying to pull, and it won't work. The answer is still no."

"All right." Abby sighed. "You're forcing me to play dirty. I don't like to put it like this, but if you come with me tonight, I'll also promise not to tell your mom who put the earthworms in her freezer."

Heather gasped. "You wouldn't!"

"I wouldn't want to," Abby agreed, "but I'm desperate, Heather. If I don't find that doll, I don't know what I'll do!"

Heather stared at her for a long moment. Then her shoulders slumped. "Okay," she said. "So give me the details."

Abby clapped her on the back. "Way to go, Heather," she said. "I knew you wouldn't let me down. How about if you invite me over after supper to work on our science project? Then we could say we want to walk to the drugstore for ice cream. Julie's house isn't too far from yours, so we'll have plenty of time to search. How does that sound?"

"Scary," Heather answered. "Something tells me this is going to be one night I'll never forget."

Chapter Six

Into the Closet

The evening shadows were already dark puddles on the sidewalks as Abby and Heather made their way toward Julie's house.

"We'll have to hurry," Heather urged. "I don't like the idea of being out after dark, especially inside someone else's house."

"Relax," Abby said, trying not to show that she was as nervous as her friend. "If the doll's in Julie's house, it shouldn't be that hard to find. It will probably be right out in plain sight, on her bed, maybe. With that big a family, who notices things like that? All we'll have to do is sneak in, grab my doll, and sneak right back out again."

"Without getting caught!" Heather reminded her. "That's the part that bothers me. When Julie finds out that the doll's gone, what will she do?"

"What *can* she do? She stole the doll in the first place," Abby pointed out. "She couldn't go to the police about it, could she? I'm telling you, Heather, it's not going to be that hard. Give me a break and stop moaning about it, okay?"

But Heather still looked unhappy as they rounded the corner onto Poplar Street. The Wise family lived in a little gray house at the end of the block.

"There it is," said Abby, as the house

came into view. "Gosh, what a mess! It looks as if they haven't mowed the yard in ten years."

"At least," Heather agreed. "And the house doesn't look any better. When do you suppose it had its last coat of paint?"

"I've heard Julie's family doesn't have much money," Abby said, "but I never looked that closely at their house before."

"I'm leaving," Heather announced firmly. "There's no way I'm going to walk through that yard, let alone go into that house. There might be snakes or spiders or *anything* hiding in all those weeds."

Abby sighed. "We can't give up now," she said. "Not after we've come all the way over here. Look—there aren't any cars in the driveway, and all the lights are off. There's no one here to catch us. Besides, you promised, remember? Come on, Heather—just a few minutes and we'll be out of here."

"Well, at least it shouldn't be too hard to get inside," Heather muttered as the girls pushed open the rusty gate and picked their way carefully up the cracked, uneven sidewalk. "From the looks of things, if you even touched that front door, it would cave right in."

"See, what did I tell you?" Abby said. "No sweat."

The door wasn't even locked. The second Abby touched it, it swung slowly open on squeaky hinges, and the two girls stepped into a tiny, dark, cluttered hall-way.

"Probably nothing in here worth stealing, anyway," Heather said.

"Except my doll," Abby reminded her. "Have you got our flashlights in your backpack? We don't want to turn on any lights."

A few seconds later, their flashlights cut yellow beams through the darkness as they slowly picked their way from room to crowded, messy room.

"I never saw anything like this," Heather said, her voice a whisper, even though there was no one to hear. "We'll never find your doll in all this mess."

"We have to try," Abby whispered back. "It would help if we could find Julie's bedroom."

"Let's try upstairs," Heather suggested. "The bedrooms are probably up there."

"Well, this can't be it," Abby announced a minute later as they stood in the doorway of the first upstairs bedroom. "There are boys' clothes all over the floor, and that looks like a baseball uniform thrown over the top of the closet door. It must be her brothers' room."

"Maybe Julie's room is across the hall." Heather turned a doorknob and shone her flashlight into the room. "Yeah, this must be it. At least, those are girls' clothes tossed on the beds. Gosh, Abby, Julie and all her sisters must sleep in this one room. There are four beds in here!"

"Never mind," Abby said impatiently, squeezing into the doorway beside her friend. "Do you see Desi?"

Their flashlights darted here and there, around the messy room.

"Wait!" cried Heather. "There she is—on top of that chest of drawers."

"Desi!" Abby squealed, rushing across the room to grab her doll. "I was right, Heather. Julie *did* take her!"

"I'm glad we found her," Heather agreed. "But let's hurry and get out of here now, please, Abby. If I have to stay in this place one more minute, my skin will crawl right off my bones. Besides, it really is dark now. The ball game should be over, and the Wises will probably be back any minute."

"You're right," Abby nodded. "Besides, your folks will—"

"Abby!" Heather clutched her friend's arm. "Look out the window. Car lights! There's a car turning into the driveway. The Wises are home." In the glow of the flashlight, her face suddenly looked white.

Abby's teeth began to chatter. "Oh, no," she moaned, "why now? In two minutes, we would have been gone."

"Well, we don't have time to stand here and talk about it," Heather snapped. "What do we do now?"

Frantically, Abby looked around the cluttered room. "Hide!" she whispered. "In Julie's closet—quick. I just heard the front door open!"

The two girls rushed into the tiny closet, closing the door as the first footsteps creaked on the stairs.

"They're coming up here!" Heather whispered. "What will we do if someone comes into this room?"

"Shhhh," Abby hissed. "And turn off your flashlight. They'll see the light under the door."

Heather flicked the switch of her flashlight, plunging the girls into blackness. Abby could feel Heather trembling, and her own knees weren't very steady. Holding her breath, Abby waited.

"I didn't either take a bite of your stupid ice-cream cone!" The bedroom light clicked on, and the girls recognized Julie's shrill, angry voice. "If you had been paying attention to what you were doing, you wouldn't have dropped the dumb thing. Now leave me alone so I can do my homework."

"You did too eat my ice cream," Julie's little sister whined. "I'm going to tell Dad, and he'll punish you, wait and see."

"Oh, shut up," Julie muttered. "Have you seen my spelling book? I left it right here on the— Hey! Where is it, you little creep? What did you do with my new doll?"

In the closet, Abby and Heather held their breaths as Julie's voice rose to a loud, furious shriek.

"I know one of you little brats took my doll. Now tell me where it is, or you'll be sorry."

"Hey!" The girls heard a man's voice, gruff and angry. "What's going on in here? I can't even hear the TV for all the racket.

Pipe down, you girls, before I have to *make* you. What's all the ruckus about, any-way?"

"She took my new doll," Julie sputtered. "It had to be either her or April. I just got that doll, and I want it back."

"What new doll?" Now Mr. Wise's voice sounded suspicious. "We didn't get you no new doll. Where did you get anything like that?"

Then a new voice chimed in, just as loud and shrill as Julie's. Julie's mom, Abby thought, huddling with Heather in the darkness of the closet.

"Yeah, where'd you get a doll? You don't have enough money to be buyin' nothin' fancy like dolls."

Julie mumbled something Abby couldn't hear.

"Speak up," her dad roared. "We asked you a question, girl, and you're going to answer if we have to stand here all night. Now, where did you get a doll?"

"In the dump," Julie repeated, her voice tearful. "I found it in the city dump, all right? It wasn't too dirty, so I cleaned it up and brought it home. It was a great doll, and one of the brats stole it. Why are you picking on me? Why don't you ask them what—"

"Now you hush, girl!" Julie's dad shouted. "If you expect me to believe that story, you're crazy! You swiped that doll from someone, and don't think I don't know it."

"No, I didn't, Dad, honest," Julie whined. "If you'll just give me a chance to explain—"

"Oh, you'll explain, all right!" her dad barked. "You'll explain at the end of my belt, if you aren't careful."

"Better tell the truth, Julie," her mother said. "You don't want your dad to spank you, do you?"

"No, Dad!" Julie begged. "No, Mom! Please, just wait a minute—"

"No more waitin'!" Julie's dad shouted. "I'm going to spank you right now, you little thief."

A moment later, Abby and Heather heard the frantic scrabbling of Julie's running shoes, followed by the pounding of her parents' and sister's shoes as they ran from the room. *Thud, thud, thud, thud,* they all rushed down the stairs. Then, from downstairs, there was an excited babbling of voices as Julie's brothers and other sisters asked what was going on.

"Poor Julie!" Heather whispered shakily. "You—you don't suppose they're really going to spank her, do you?"

"I—I don't know," Abby admitted. "We can't be caught here now, Heather. Maybe we can sneak out the front door while they're all busy down there."

"I'm afraid," Heather answered, trembling more than ever. "What if they see us?"

"We'll just have to run faster than they do," Abby said, trying to sound braver than she felt. "Come on, let's get out of here while the getting's good."

Quickly, they slipped from the closet and tiptoed hurriedly toward the bedroom door. They hardly dared to breathe as they tiptoed down the stairs, stopping on the bottom step to peer around the hall doorway.

"I don't see anyone," Abby whispered. "It sounds like they're all back in the kitchen. Quick, Heather—run for it!"

A moment later they had torn open the front door, letting it bang shut behind them, and taken the porch steps in a single jump.

Abby held her doll tightly against her hammering heart as they ran block after block in the dim light of the streetlamps. It was only when they reached Heather's front yard that they dared to slow down. Gasping for air, they leaned against the porch railing until the stitches in their sides had disappeared and they could breathe again.

"I've never been so scared in my life," Heather wheezed, sinking down onto the porch steps. "I can't believe I let you get me into such a mess."

"Me, either," Abby admitted, still shaking. Then her face brightened. "On the other hand," she reminded Heather, "we did get Desi back. And that's what we went over there for, right?"

"But what's going to happen to Julie?" Heather asked. "I can't help worrying about her, even if she did take your doll. Her family's terrible."

"That's the word, all right," Abby agreed. "But I don't know what we could have done to help. And I'm sure she'll be okay. She's lived with them all her life, remember?"

"I hope you're right." Heather sighed. "But I'm really worried."

Both girls were silent, staring down at Abby's doll, who smiled mysteriously up at them in the glow of the porch light.

Chapter Seven

Where's Julie?

"A friend in need is a friend indeed, that's what some people say. You know someone who needs a friend, and needs a friend today!"

"What's that all about?" Heather demanded as the girls walked up the front steps of the school the next morning, with Sandy trailing behind.

"Desi's been saying weird stuff like that all morning," Abby's little sister piped up. "I didn't know dolls ever said stuff like that."

Abby and Heather exchanged glances. "Desi's not like other dolls, you know that," Abby reminded her sister. "She's special. Why shouldn't a one-of-a-kind doll say one-of-a-kind things?"

"I still think it's weird," Sandy insisted as she paused in the doorway of the second-grade room. "She keeps talking about friends, friends, friends—maybe her record got stuck."

"Maybe," Abby agreed as her little sister disappeared into her classroom. But the second Sandy was gone, she turned to Heather, her forehead puckered in a frown. "I still haven't told Sandy about Desi's special gifts. But Sandy's right," she told Heather, "that's all Desi's talked about today—friend this and friend that. I think she's trying to tell me something, but I can't figure out what."

Heather shrugged. "Does everything she says have to mean something? After all, she is just a doll. Maybe sometimes she talks just to talk."

"Maybe," Abby admitted. "All the same, it makes me feel kind of funny. Remember when she told you not to go into our basement? What if there's something we need to know now? What if we don't figure it out in time?"

"In time for what?" Heather asked. "You're imagining things, Abby. Calm down. You're still just shook up about what happened last night. You know, over at Julie's house."

Abby shuddered, remembering. "Maybe that's it," she agreed. "Still, I'll be glad when Desi gets off the subject. I'm getting sick of all this stuff about friends."

It wasn't until Miss Applegate took morning roll call that Abby noticed Julie wasn't at her desk by the window. She wasn't lunch monitor this week, so she couldn't be taking the lunch money to the office. And it wasn't her turn to clean the erasers on the school porch. Where could she be?

Maybe Julie was sick, Abby decided, opening her notebook to take out her math homework. But she had seemed okay the night before. Maybe—

No, Abby told herself. Don't be silly. Julie's okay, you know she is. The worst thing that could have happened to her was a spanking, wasn't it? But her folks were awfully mad . . .

She looked out of the corner of her eye and saw Heather looking back at her. By the worried expression on Heather's face, her friend was having the same crazy thoughts.

But this is stupid, Abby told herself. Julie's missed school before, and you didn't worry about it. Everyone misses school sometimes. Why not Julie?

All the same, she caught herself staring at Julie's empty desk several times during that long, long morning. It had never

69

seemed like such a long wait for the recess bell.

The minute the bell rang, Abby grabbed her doll, and she and Heather hurried to the far corner of the playground, where they could talk.

"Are you thinking what I'm thinking?" Heather demanded, the second they were alone.

"I don't know what to think," Abby said. "I thought I wanted Julie to be punished. But her father was so mad, maybe he really hurt her. Nothing could actually have happened to Julie, could it?"

"Why don't you ask Desi?" Heather suggested. "Maybe that's what she's been trying to tell you all day."

Abby stared at her friend. "Aren't you the one who said that Desi was 'just a doll'?" she asked.

"Forget what I said," Heather said. "Just ask her."

"Okay, okay," Abby grumbled, "but as long as her folks didn't actually *hurt* her, I

70

think Julie deserved to be scolded. That was a dirty trick, stealing my doll and telling her parents she found it in the dump."

Just thinking about that made Abby scowl as she pulled the ring on the back of Desi's neck. "And you'd better not give me any more of that 'friendship' stuff, either," she warned the doll. "I'm not Julie's friend, and I never will be."

Whir, hum . . . "No one can see her, no one will know. She's lost and in trouble, so please don't be slow!"

Abby almost dropped the doll. A cold feeling tingled at the back of her neck as she stared into Desi's blue eyes.

"What was *that* all about?" she demanded.

Heather's face looked greenish, as if she were about to lose her breakfast. "I—I don't know," she whispered. "But I don't like the sound of it. Abby, maybe Julie's in danger. Maybe we'd better *do* something."

Abby made herself laugh, although her throat suddenly felt dry and tight. "Maybe

71

we're just being silly," she said. "Her parents were mad, but my folks get mad, too, sometimes. That doesn't mean they'd really do anything to her. Besides, even if we wanted to help, what could we do?"

"We could tell Miss Applegate," Heather suggested. "She'd know what to do."

Abby lost her patience. "Whose friend are you, anyway, mine or Julie's?" she snapped. "She took *my* doll, remember? We'd get in trouble with our folks if we stole something like that, so why shouldn't she?"

"I don't know . . ." Heather began, but just then the bell rang, and they had to run for the building.

Abby didn't even take Desi with her to afternoon recess. If Julie were in trouble, she didn't want the doll nagging her about it. After all, Julie got what she deserved.

Chapter Eight

To the Rescue

Just the same, when Heather suggested that they stop by Julie's house after school, Abby didn't argue. "Okay, okay, anything to make you quit talking about it," she muttered as they opened the rusty gate and picked their way through the overgrown, cluttered yard.

Five minutes later, all their knocking,

yelling, and pounding on the door had left them hoarse and tired. There was still no sign of Julie, or any of the rest of the family.

"I don't get it," Heather said. "If Julie were sick enough to stay home from school, where is she now?"

"Maybe she went to the doctor," Abby suggested. "Or maybe—"

"Hey, kids!"

The girls whirled around to see an old woman in a faded housedress leaning on the fence beside the Wise house.

"Are you looking for one of the Wise kids?" the woman asked. "Because if you are, I can tell you, you're not going to find them. Not a one of 'em home. I never saw such coming and going, with the police cars and all—"

"Police!" Abby's heart stopped beating for a second or two. "What were the police doing here? Did something happen to one of the Wises?"

"Guess you could say that," the woman

said. "It's that girl, the one who's about your age, I guess. You know, she's always wearing pink."

"Julie!" Abby and Heather gasped together.

Abby squeezed her doll more tightly as she stammered, "Wh-what happened to Julie? Did she get sick? Is she hurt?"

The old woman shrugged. "Who knows?" she said. "Fact is, her mother told me, the kid was gone when the family got up this morning. They haven't seen hide nor hair of her all day. Looks as if she ran away—and no one knows where to look for her."

"Ran away!" Heather groaned. "Oh, Abby, I told you something was wrong!"

Abby tried to speak calmly. "Let's not jump to any conclusions," she said. "Everyone runs away at least once. Remember when we were five and ran away because our folks wouldn't take us to the circus?"

"That was different, and you know it," Heather argued. "We just went down the block and had cookies at Mrs. Ramsey's house. We were back home before our mothers even knew we were gone. Julie's been missing all day! Besides, you know what Desi—"

"Shh," Abby interrupted, glancing at the Wises' neighbor. "Later, Heather. Come on, let's get out of here. We can—we can talk to Desi when we're back at my house."

As soon as they were out of the old woman's sight, the girls began to run. They didn't stop until they were upstairs in Abby's bedroom. They threw themselves down on her bed and looked at each other with wide, scared eyes.

"I still say it's nothing to worry about," Abby insisted stubbornly. "Besides—"

"I don't care what you say, I'm worried anyway," Heather said. "And you can't fool me—I know you're worried, too. Even if Julie took your doll, she doesn't deserve to get hurt. Quick, Abby, pull Desi's string. If anyone knows what's happened to Julie, it's your doll."

"Okay, okay," Abby grumbled, "but I still say this is silly. Julie can take care of herself."

Just the same, her hand shook a little as she pulled the doll's string. She and Heather both held their breath, waiting for the mechanical voice.

"Julie has vanished, just like a breeze. You can't see the forest because of the trees."

"What does *that* mean?" Heather asked.

Abby shrugged. "Who knows? I wish just once Desi would say what she means, instead of talking in riddles."

"Try again," Heather suggested. "If we have enough hints, maybe we can figure out where Julie's gone."

Abby pulled the string. Whir, hum . . . "Red on the grass, red on the stone—nobody hears her, she's all alone!"

Heather frowned. "Red . . ." she mur-

mured. Then she gasped. "Abby, I don't like the sound of that. Could—could Desi mean *blood*? Could Julie be hurt out there somewhere?"

Abby chewed on her lower lip, thinking as fast as she could. "Red," she repeated. "Stone, grass. What else did she say? Something about trees and a forest—"

"Rhymer's Woods!" Heather cried, jumping to her feet. "Abby, I'll bet anything that Julie is in Rhymer's Woods, and something's happened to her."

"We have to find her," Abby whispered. "Oh, Heather, if you're right, we have to find Julie. It may already be too late!"

The girls rushed for the door. As they threw it open, they bumped into Sandy standing in the doorway. She was stuffing cookies into her mouth.

"Where are you going?" she demanded. "I want to come, too."

"No way," Abby said, pushing past her sister. "This is important. You'd slow us down."

"Would not!" Sandy argued. "Besides, if you don't let me come with you, I'll tell Mom. She'll *make* you take me."

"Listen, Sandy—" Abby began, but Heather interrupted.

"For pete's sake, let her come," she said. "We're losing time standing here arguing with her. But you'll have to keep up, Sandy. This could be a matter of life and death. Every minute counts."

"Watch me." Sandy grinned.

A minute later, all three girls were on their bikes, with Desi in Abby's bike basket, pedaling toward the woods on the south edge of town.

"If she's in the woods, it could take forever to find her," Heather shouted, as they raced along. "Rhymer's Woods is such a big, dark place."

"Who?" Sandy yelled, struggling to keep up. "*Who* is in the woods?"

"A friend of ours," Abby yelled back. "No talking, Sandy. You'd better use all your breath for pedaling."

In just a few minutes, they were following the railroad tracks past the last few houses at the very edge of town. The woods were still a dark blur on the horizon as they pedaled past fences and pastures and a few sleepy-looking cows.

"I hope we're right about the woods," Abby said. "It would be awful if we wasted a lot of time looking in the wrong place."

Heather groaned and braked her bike to a standstill in the middle of the dusty road. "You're right," she said, "but how can we tell?"

"What's going *on?*" Sandy whined. "Will someone please tell me why we're here?"

"There's only one thing to do," Abby said, ignoring her little sister. "We have to ask Desi. Desi will know."

"Ask Desi?" Sandy stared at her. "You're talking crazy, Abby. Why do you want to ask Desi anything? She's a *doll!*"

"Just listen," Abby said, "we don't have time to explain now, but we'll tell everything later, I promise."

Abby pulled her doll from the bike basket and quickly flipped it over, tugging on the ring in Desi's neck. Whir, hum . . .

"You're heading for just the right place, don't worry—time's growing short, so don't stand there—please hurry!"

"Quick, guys!" Heather urged, jumping back onto her bike. "We don't have time to stand here and talk!"

"At least we know we're going in the right direction," Abby said as they rushed off again.

The wind ripped at their hair and slapped at their faces as they tore down the deserted country road toward Rhymer's Woods.

"We'd better ditch our bikes and go in on foot," Abby shouted as they reached the edge of the forest. "We can't ride through all that brush."

The three girls dropped their bikes by the edge of the road and scrambled over the roadside ditch, skinning their hands and ripping the knees of their jeans on

sharp rocks. They looked into the dark, gloomy woods and stood still, hardly daring to breathe. Then—

"Look!" cried Heather. "Down there —do you see something pink?"

Sure enough, something small and pink blew in the wind, caught in the thorny bushes.

"It's a hair ribbon!" Sandy said, as they reached it.

"*Julie's* hair ribbon," Abby added. "She *did* come this way! But where is she now?"

They strained their eyes as far into the woods as they could see, but there was no sign of Julie.

"Like it or not, we're going to have to go in there," said Abby with a sigh.

"But Mom told us never to go into Rhymer's Woods," Sandy protested. "She said there are snakes in there. If she finds out, she'll ground us for the rest of our lives."

Abby took a deep breath. "I don't think we have much choice," she said. "Not if

Julie's in trouble somewhere in there. Come on, guys, let's just do it."

The darkness of the forest seemed to close about them like a cold hand. They took a deep breath and stepped into the trees.

Chapter Nine

Just in Time

The farther they pressed into the woods, the darker it got, until the girls could hardly see to put one shoe in front of the other. The tall old trees grew so close together that their branches tangled overhead, shutting off all but a weak trickle of afternoon sunlight. Vines and creepers snaked across the narrow path, catching at their feet, and little branches whipped at their faces as they pushed forward. There was hardly a sound in the forest. Even the breeze seemed to be holding its breath, listening for Julie.

"Julie!" Abby called, peering through the shadows. "Julie, where are you? Can you hear us?"

Sandy shuddered and pressed closer to her big sister. "I don't like it here," she complained. "Why do you guys think Julie is in the woods? No one ever comes here— it's too spooky."

"We'll explain all that later," Heather promised. "For now, just help us look, okay?"

"Maybe we should be watching for crushed grass and broken branches," Abby suggested. "You know, the way they taught us in Scouts. Julie couldn't have gone very far into this mess without leaving some kind of trail."

"That's a good idea," Heather agreed. "I have to keep my eyes on the ground, anyway, just to keep from falling."

Fifteen minutes later, Sandy spotted a trampled place in the path. It looked as if someone had lain down in the brown, dry leaves that had drifted there.

"She must have stopped here to rest," Abby said. "And look, there's a bubble-gum wrapper over there beside that bush. It looks new, too. I bet we're on her trail now."

"She could be miles and miles away, though," Heather said with a discouraged sigh. "And it will be dark in a couple of hours. Our folks will be worried if we're not home by then."

"We can look a little while longer," Abby decided. "And if we don't find her by the time it starts to get dark, at least we know she's here in the woods someplace. We can get help when we get back to town."

"I hope we find her by then," Heather said. "After what Desi—you know . . ."

The girls exchanged worried glances, while Sandy tagged along, demanding to know what they were talking about.

"Okay, now we can tell you," Abby said. "But you're never going to believe this, Sandy. It all started the day we went to the toy shop and bought Desi. Remember what Emily Moonbow said, about her being a special doll? Well, she didn't tell us half of it."

By the time Abby and Heather finished their story, Sandy's eyes were as big and round as silver dollars. "You're right," she said, "that is hard to believe. In fact, I don't know if I really do. But so many weird things have happened since you bought that doll, I have to think maybe you're right. And I did hear her saying something really weird this morning. Every time you pulled the string, she said something about friends. Maybe she *is* magic."

A cool breeze sprang up, making them hug their sweaters tighter around their shoulders, and the shadows were growing deeper by the minute. Soon the sun would begin to slide below the hills. If Julie were still in these woods when dark came, scared and alone and maybe hurt . . . They quickened their steps, pushing farther and farther into the trees.

"Abby!" Heather gasped suddenly, grabbing her friend's arm. "Do you see what I see? Through the trees—something pink."

Abby followed her pointing finger and began to run. That flash of pink, there on the ground beneath the trees—that had to be Julie's faded old sweatshirt.

The other girls were right behind Abby as she skidded to a stop beside Julie's un-moving body. Julie lay absolutely still in the dark shadow of a huge oak tree, her face white and her eyes closed. And there on a rock beside her head was a little pool of something red. The girls didn't have to look twice to know it was blood.

"She must have fallen and hit her head," Abby said.

"Is—is she dead?" Sandy asked, her voice sounding little and scared.

"No," Heather reassured her quickly, "she's breathing, see? You can see her chest go up and down."

"We have to get help quick," Abby said. "I don't want to leave her alone, though. Why don't you two run back to our bikes and ride to that farm we passed down the road? They'd let you use their phone to call an ambulance. I'll stay here with Julie, in case she wakes up."

Sandy hesitated. "But what if we get lost?" she wailed.

"You won't," Abby promised her. "Just stay on the path, and you'll come out right where we went into the trees. Just—just hurry, okay? I don't want to be here when it gets dark."

"We can do it," Heather said. "Don't worry, Sandy, I'll be right with you. And Abby's right. Julie needs an ambulance. She could be badly hurt."

Sandy swallowed hard. "Okay," she said,

"if you promise not to let us get separated. We'll hurry, Abby. You and Julie just hang in there, all right?"

As Sandy and Heather disappeared down the trail, Abby sighed and turned to where Julie was lying on the ground. She knew better than to move her. In Scouts, she had learned never to move someone with a head injury. But Julie looked so cold on the damp ground. Every few minutes, a shiver rippled through her thin body. Abby took off her sweater and laid it across Julie, tucking it in around her as tightly as she could.

Then she sat down to wait, leaning against the rough bark of an ancient tree, never taking her eyes from Julie for a second. She hugged Desi a little closer in her arms, glad to have her doll's company.

She hoped Heather and Sandy would hurry. Julie wasn't looking too good.

Julie's hospital room was cool and white and smelled like medicine. But Abby hardly noticed the smell as she, Heather, and Sandy stood beside the high, railed bed, looking down at Julie's pale face. A thick white bandage covered most of Julie's forehead, but she was smiling up at them.

"I don't know how to thank you guys," she said weakly. "The doctor told my mom and dad you found me just in time. I could have died if I'd been out there much longer."

"It's okay," Heather told her. "But we never would have known where to find you if it hadn't been for Abby's doll."

Julie shook her head, wincing a little. "I still have trouble believing that," she said. "A magic doll! I never heard of anything like that. But you found me, all right, so I guess I can't argue. Now I feel worse than ever that I took her from you in the first place."

Tears began to streak down her face, and her mouth started to shake.

"Dad spanked me the other night," she said, in such a soft voice that they could hardly hear her. "He yells a lot, but he's never done anything like that before. I was scared to stay home. So yesterday morning, before anyone else was awake, I decided to run away. I didn't expect to fall and hit my stupid head on a rock. Trust me to do something dumb like that."

Abby stared at her, her heart sinking lower and lower, until it felt as if it would sink right down into her running shoes.

"I'm sorry," she whispered, "I didn't know it was that bad for you, honest."

"How could you know?" Julie sighed, wiping one hand across her tear-streaked face. "It's not like you guys are my friends, or anything. Who'd expect you to know?"

"But we are," Heather said suddenly. "We are your friends, Julie. At least—I'd like to be."

"Me, too," Abby agreed. "We've been pretty lousy friends so far, I guess, but we'll do better, if you'll just give us a chance."

Julie stared first at Abby, then at Heather, grinning over the rails of the hospital bed.

Chapter Ten

Friends

"When I think about that day in the woods, it still makes my stomach hurt," Abby admitted as the four girls walked down the road.

"So don't think about it," Julie answered with a shudder. "I know *I* try not to."

"But I can't help it," Abby said. "What if

Desi hadn't told us where you were? What if we hadn't listened to her?"

"That's the part I still can't believe," Sandy chimed in. "A magic doll. Who ever heard of anything like that?"

"And just think—I'm going to get a doll of my very own." Julie gave a happy little skip. "It was really great of you guys to set up that lemonade stand to help me earn the money. I never had a doll before—not a new one, anyway. And not one as pretty as Desi."

"That's okay," Abby answered. "We all had fun with the lemonade stand. And I want to go back to the toy store. I have some questions for Emily Moonbow. I want to know about Desi—what kind of doll she is, and why that woman insisted I had to buy her. Until I know, I'll never stop thinking about it. I have to try to understand, at least."

"That's right," Heather agreed. "I think Emily Moonbow knew something was going to happen all along. Remember, she

said Desi might tell you something you
needed to know."

"And there's another weird thing, too,"
Abby said. "Do you know we're the only
people who have ever been in that toy
shop? A bunch of the other kids tried, but
it was closed every time they went."

"Well, we'll just keep knocking until she
comes to the door," Julie said. "If anyone
knows what really happened, it's got to be
her. And I think she owes us an explanation."

But when they got to the little shop
where Abby had bought the Friendship
Doll, they saw right away that something
was different.

"The windows," Sandy pointed out.
"They're all empty. Weren't there dolls and
toys in the windows the last time we were
here?"

"And the 'Open' sign is gone from the
front door, too," Heather said.

"But the sign out front is still there,"
Abby noticed, pointing to the heart-shaped

sign with its wreaths of ribbons and flow-ers around the fancy pink letters that spelled out the name of the shop: Heart's Desire.

"We'll never know anything just stand-ing here," Julie said. "Come on, let's knock."

Although they knocked until their knuckles were sore and rang the doorbell at least a dozen times, there was no an-swer.

"I think she's gone," Sandy said, cup-ping her hands around her eyes to peer through the front window. "There's not a single toy in there, see?"

Sure enough, not a doll, not a game, not a teddy bear remained. There was only the bare, sunny living room, and one shred of pink ribbon in the middle of the empty floor.

"But where could she have gone?" Heather demanded. "She just opened this shop a few weeks ago."

"It's almost as if—" Abby shook her

head, afraid she would sound silly. "It's almost as if she only stayed here long enough to sell this one doll. As if—as if that were her plan all along."

The four girls stared at each other, feeling a sudden chill even on this sunny day.

"How did a doll know about me?" Julie reached out to stroke Desi's golden hair. "How did she know I would run away and get hurt in the woods?"

"She knew, that's all," Abby answered.

"Remember what the lady said?" Sandy asked. "She said you would find a friend in her shop. And you did. Desi is a lot more than just a doll."

Abby looked down at the doll in her arms. "She helped me get to know you, too, Julie," she said. "I guess I really found *two* friends when I bought Desi."

"Thanks, Abby." Julie smiled. Then she gave a little sigh. "All the same, I'm really disappointed. Now I'll never have a doll like Desi."

"There *is* no other doll like Desi," Abby

reminded her. "She's a one-of-a-kind." For a moment, she hugged her doll tightly in her arms. Then she held it out to Julie. "Here," she said, "Desi can be your doll, too."

Julie's eyes widened. "Really?" She gasped. "You're giving her to *me*?"

"Well, only part-time," Abby explained. "I thought we could all take turns keeping her. That way it will kind of be like she belongs to all of us."

Julie looked longingly at the golden-haired doll. Then she shook her head. "Desi is yours," she said. "If I really want a doll, I can use my money to buy one next time my folks go to the city. Besides, I don't need a doll for a friend now. I have *real* friends—all of you guys."

As they laughed, Heather reached out to straighten the folds of Desi's filmy skirts. "I wonder if she'll keep on saying strange things, now that she's done what she came to do?" she said.

Reaching for the doll's string, she pulled

it and heard the usual whir and hum, then the doll's scratchy voice. "I'm here to be your friend, you see, so won't you come and play with me?"

"That sounds like any other doll," Heather said. "In fact, I haven't heard her say anything weird since that day in the woods. Maybe all the magic is used up now, Abby."

Abby hugged her doll. "Maybe," she said. "Or maybe it's just waiting. You know—until the next time we need it. Maybe someday the magic will come back again."

The tiny silver bells on Desi's dress tinkled gently, and her big blue eyes seemed to glow with a mysterious light.

Maybe someday, they seemed to promise.

Maybe someday . . .